The Adventures of Sancho and Bessie

Samantha Pitts & Vidya Vasudevan

This book is dedicated to my grandfather, for without him these cows would not exist.

Sancho and Bessie, adventurous cows.
Sancho is spotted and Bessie is brown.

The pair left the barn. They were ready to play.
They went out with the plan to be gone for the day.

Sancho told Bessie, "Let's head to the hollow".
Bessie replied, "If you lead I will follow".
Sancho led Bessie along the tree line.
Down the steep path, now who knows what they'll find.

The promise of grass, so soft under hoof,
Kept curious Sancho and Bessie on the move.

Up on a branch, do you see what they see?
Hootie the owl is there, up in the tree.

"If you go right, to the right there is danger.
Coyote is there and he meets no stranger."

The grumpy old owl then flew up high.
The cows waved at owl, and the wise bird said goodbye.

As they went down the path the cows heard a soft hiss.
It sounded exciting and something like thisssss!

It was Stevie the snake, and without much to say
The snake slithered on and was out of the way.

They followed the river away from the snake.
Then jumped in the water, oh boy it felt great!

Living in the water was a stinky green toad.
He told the cows to hit the road.

Sancho and Bessie then saw something odd.
He looked at her, and gave a big nod.
They both made a gulp as they stared at the cave.
Sancho told Bessie, "Lets go and be brave".

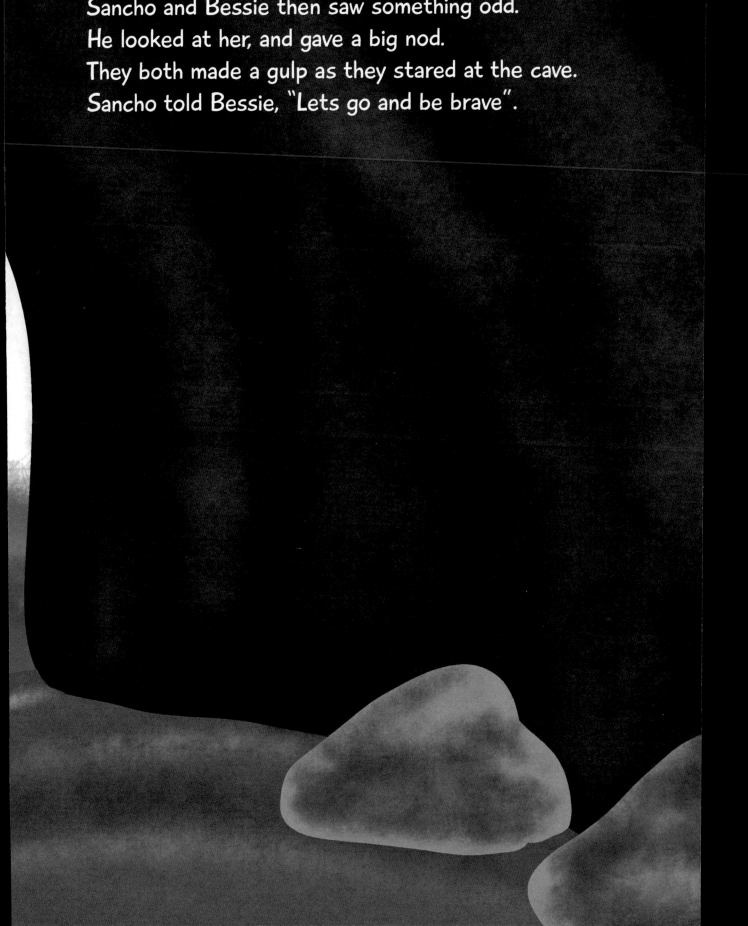

They entered the cave with long hesitation,
Surprised and amazed by their own observation.
So many fun colors, they could not deny,
This cave has a rainbow of bats that can fly!

Yellow and blue bats, and green, even gold.
Bats that were purple, so royal and bold.

They winked at the cows and they put on a show,
Flying through cracks and swooping down low.

The cows jumped and played. In the bat cave they tumbled.
Their tummies were empty and started to rumble.
The cows got so hungry, but they had no snacks.
It was time for their breakfast so they headed back.

"No time for the hollow," poor Bessie replied.
The cows had a race and it took them big strides.
They ran from those bats and back home through the trees,
They jumped the low fence with grace and ease.

Sancho and Bessie arrived at the barn.
If cows miss their breakfast they think they will starve!
The table was set with their favorite hot meal.
A plate of fresh flapjacks, the smell was unreal.

Sancho and Bessie loved pancakes so much.
Their pancakes were spotted and soft to the touch.

Hot maple syrup and creamy gold butter,
Adventure makes breakfast a meal like none other.

And they ate every last yummy bite.

The end.

ABOUT THE AUTHOR:

Samantha Pitts was raised outside the small town of Cordele, GA. She grew up listening to tall tales about two cows from her mother Dorothy Drinnon. These stories were passed down from Dorothy's father, James Hansel Pate. Samantha continued the tradition with her own son, and felt that these stories deserved to be shared with everyone.

The Adventures of Sancho and Bessie is Samantha's first children's book.

Made in the USA
Columbia, SC
12 November 2021